MARC BROWN

ARTHUR'S TOOTH

LITTLE, BROWN AND COMPANY

New York Boston

For Ralph Sozio, S.D. (*Super Dentist*)

Little, Brown and Company
Hachette Book Group
1290 Avenue of the Americas, New York, NY 10104
Visit our website at www.lb-kids.com

Little, Brown and Company is a division of Hachette Book Group, Inc.
The Little, Brown name and logo are trademarks of Hachette Book Group, Inc.

The publisher is not responsible for websites (or their content) that are not owned by the publisher.

First Revised Edition: June 2011
First published in hardcover in September 1985 by Little, Brown and Company

Arthur® is a registered trademark of Marc Brown.

Library of Congress Cataloging-in-Publication Data

Brown, Marc Tolon.
Arthur's tooth / Marc Brown.—1st ed.
p. cm.
Summary: Arthur, tired of being the only one in his class who still has all his baby teeth, waits impatiently for his loose tooth to fall out.
ISBN 978-0-316-11245-1 (hc) / ISBN 978-0-316-11246-8 (pb)
[1. Children's stories, American—Fiction. 2. Teeth—Fiction.]
I. Title
PZ7.B81618Aru   1991
[E]   84-72092

30

APS

Printed in China

Finally, Arthur had a loose tooth.
He wiggled it with his tongue.
He wiggled it with his finger.
He wiggled it all the time.

One afternoon while Arthur was wiggling his tooth during math, he heard a loud scream. Francine jumped up.

"My tooth just fell out on my desk!" she cried.
"Class, how many of you have lost a tooth?"
asked Mr. Marco.
Everyone but Arthur raised their hands.

When Arthur got home, he didn't want any milk
and cookies.
"What's the matter, Arthur?" his mother asked.
"I'm the only one in my class who still has
all his baby teeth," he complained.

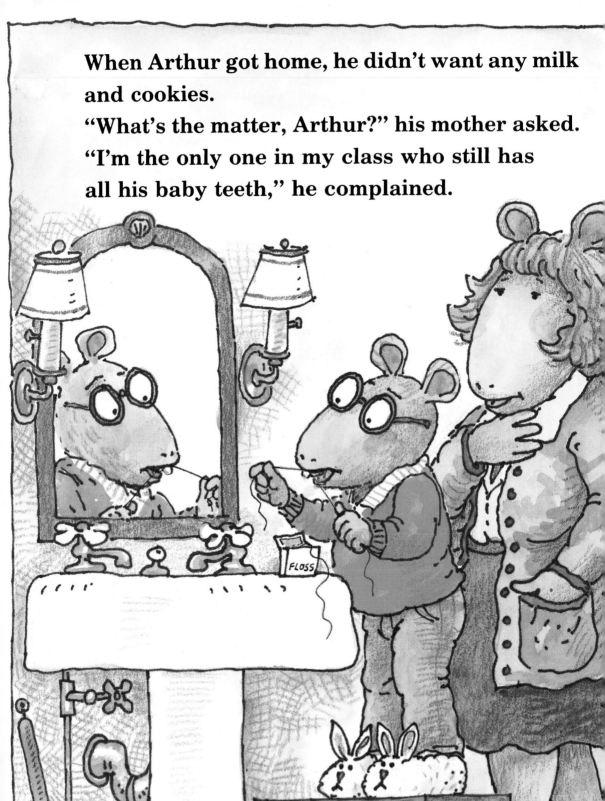

"Don't worry," said his sister, D.W. "Before you know it, all your teeth will fall out and you can get false teeth like Grandma Thora."

Arthur persuaded Father to make a special dinner for him: steak, corn on the cob, and peanut brittle.
"I can't believe one little tooth can take so long to fall out," said Father.

The next day, Muffy brought in a whole jar of her teeth for show-and-tell.

"I got two dollars for each one," she said.

"One from my dad and one from my mom. I put it all in the bank to earn interest. I'm waiting for my investment to double."

"Not me," said Francine. "I'm spending mine."

Later the class saw a movie
called *Nasty Mr. Tooth Decay.*
"Between the ages of four and seven,"
the announcer began, "everyone begins to lose
their deciduous, or baby, teeth."
"Everyone except Arthur!" shouted Francine.
The whole class laughed.
Arthur slid down in his seat. He wiggled his
tooth as hard as he could.

In the cafeteria, Francine practiced her
new tricks.
"Look!" she said. "I can keep my teeth closed,
and still drink through a straw. And I can
squirt water, too. Everybody line up for a
squirting contest — everybody except Arthur.
Babies with baby teeth can't squirt water."

By the next day, Arthur was convinced his loose
tooth would never fall out.
His friends tried to help.
Buster brought carrots
for Arthur's lunch.

Sue Ellen showed Arthur how to put raisins over his
teeth to make it look as if some were missing.

The Brain invented a special machine.
"It's a tooth remover," he explained.
"Just put your head in here."

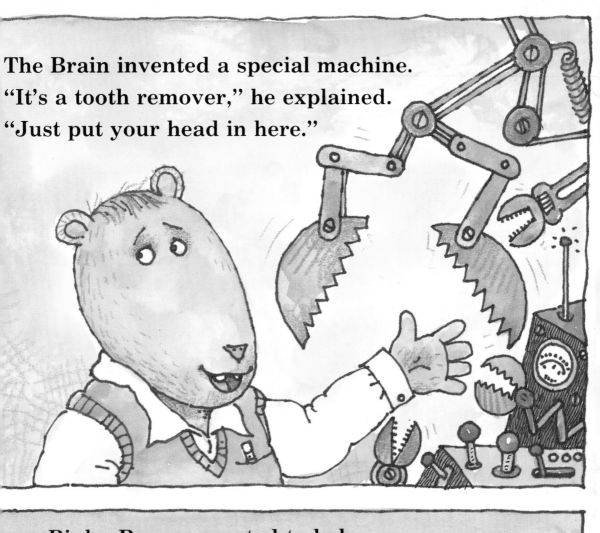

ven Binky Barnes wanted to help.
I can knock that tooth out in one second flat," he said.

That night Arthur spent a lot of time in front of the bathroom mirror.

He got up very early the next mornin
to wiggle his tooth again.
"See how much looser it is!"
he told his parents.
"That's it," said his mother.
"You need professional help.
You're going to the dentist.
Today."

There were other patients waiting to see
Dr. Sozio.
"Sorry," said the nurse. "We're running late.
Have a seat."
"Arthur, you were smart to bring a book,"
said Mother.

Finally it was Arthur's turn.

"I wish all my patients were as good at waiting as you are," said Dr. Sozio. "How old are you now, Arthur?"

"Seven," said Arthur. "And I still have all my baby teeth."

"I was eight before I lost my first tooth," said Dr. Sozio. "Everyone is different."

"Really?" said Arthur.

Dr. Sozio examined Arthur's loose tooth. "This one should fall out very soon," he said. "Just wait."

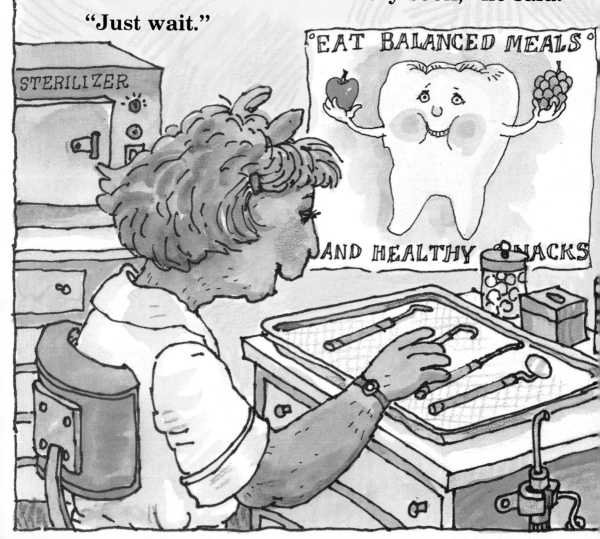

Arthur got back to school just in time for recess. "Still have all your baby teeth?" Francine asked. "Then you can't be in the game. I'm the tooth fairy. Only people who have lost teeth can play."

"If you're the tooth fairy," said Arthur,
"I think I'll keep all my teeth. I can wait."
He started over to the softball game.

"Whoever I touch," said Francine, "loses a tooth."
She flapped her arms.
"The one who loses the most, wins."

Francine twirled around and touched Buster.

She twirled faster, and touched Sue Ellen.

Twirling even faster, she slipped and hit Arthur. "Sorry, Arthur," Francine said. "But I told you, no babies allowed."

Arthur picked up his glasses.
"It's OK," he said. "It's probably the nicest
thing you've ever done for me."
"What do you mean?" asked Francine.

Arthur just smiled.